# FIRST STEPS IN CODING

## WHAT'S A VARIABLE?

### A STORY TIME ADVENTURE!

BY KAITLYN SIU AND MARCELO BADARI

**Kane Miller**
A DIVISION OF EDC PUBLISHING

First American Edition 2022
Kane Miller, A Division of EDC Publishing

Copyright © Hodder and Stoughton, 2022
First published in Great Britain in 2022
by Wayland, an imprint of Hachette Children's Group,
part of Hodder and Stoughton, Carmelite House,
50 Victoria Embankment, London EC4Y 0DZ

www.kanemiller.com
www.myubam.com

Library of Congress Control Number: 2021937273

Printed and bound in China
1 2 3 4 5 6 7 8 9 10
ISBN: 978-1-68464-339-4

MIX
Paper from
responsible sources
FSC® C104740

# WHAT'S A VARIABLE?

Let's find out! It's story time at the library and you're invited to join super-reading-robot Flex as he writes a book all by himself. We'll have loads of fun and learn some cool coding facts. Let's get reading, super coders!

Flex is a super robot who loves
to read. With his amazing
robot brain, he can read
really fast. One day, he read
a hundred books in one hour!

Flex especially loves
to visit the library.

Today Flex is heading out on his weekly trip to the library. He can't wait to find new books to read.

When Flex arrives at the library, he can't believe his good luck! The librarian tells him that they are running a special class on how to write books.

TODAY'S STORY TIME: WRITE YOUR OWN BOOK!

Flex is excited to learn how to write his own book.

He meets the story time teacher, Type, who tells Flex that he will learn to write a book called *All About Me* using a special **computer-programming** game.

Computers can help us to write simple books!

All About Me

Type shows Flex the computer program that will help him with his book.

Hello, my name is X, and I am Y years old. I love to play Z all day long.

That sounds very strange! What are the X, Y, and Z for?

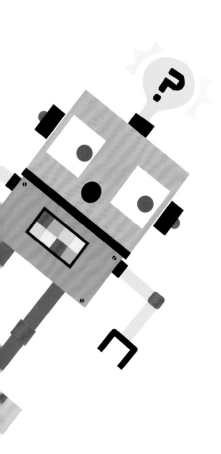

Hello, my name is X, and I am Y years old. I love to play Z all day long.

Those are awesome bits of code called variables!

A variable is like a box that keeps information inside it.

It is a way of holding this information all together. Variables can hold all kinds of things, such as numbers, letters, words – whatever we want!

Variable

# Variable

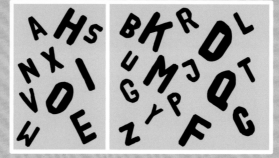

# Variable

Variables are very important for computers. These little boxes help computer programs to **access** lots of information quickly, and to make changes quickly, too.

All that amazing information inside
each variable is called a **value**.

Flex, you will write your very own
program to tell the computer what
value the variables should have in
your book! Like this:

X = Flex
Y = 13
Z = soccer

Now the computer will **replace** the variables with these values, and the book will read:

Hello,
my name is **Flex**,
and I am
**13** years old.
I love to play
**soccer** all day long.

Flex looks at the next page of the book in the programming game. The code says:

X can't wait for the big Z tournament. He only has P sleeps left!

Flex plans values for these new variables and writes the program:

X = Flex
Z = 7
P = soccer

His book now reads:

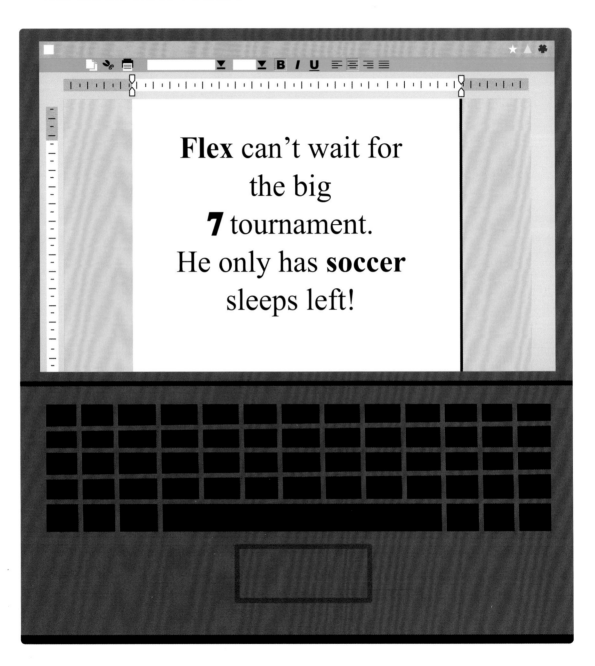

**Flex** can't wait for the big **7** tournament. He only has **soccer** sleeps left!

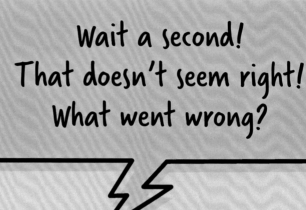

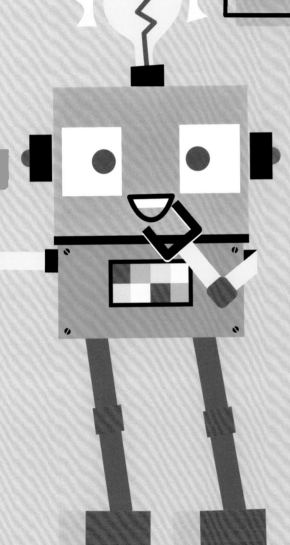

Oh no! There's a **bug** in the code!

No, not a real bug! It's a computer bug. You have to fix it, Flex. **Debug** that code!

Flex quickly sees that he mixed up the values for the Z and P variables.

No problem! Flex simply tells the computer the right values.

X = Flex
Z = soccer
P = 7

**Flex** can't wait for the big **soccer** tournament. He only has **7** sleeps left!

That looks better!

Flex's friend Volt joins him at the library. Volt loves Flex's story!

I would love to be a character in a book!

Flex knows how to change his book quickly. He changes the value for the X variable in his code.

X = Volt

The book changes before his eyes, and Volt's name appears in place of Flex's!

Hello, my name is **Volt**, and I am **13** years old. I love to play **soccer** all day long.

Wow! Changing words is easy when you use variables.

**Volt** can't wait for the big **soccer** tournament. He only has **7** sleeps left!

23

Flex's book is complete! The librarian
lets him print out one copy for Volt
and one for himself.

Flex and Volt each draw pictures
to go with the words.

Flex shows his book proudly to all his friends.

Now it's your turn! It's time to write your own story. Choose values for your variables, and read your story out loud.

Last year, I went on a **Y** trip to **X**. It was so much fun to see **Z** and **B**. **X** is a great place to visit with **P**. My favorite part of the trip was **U**.

Now for some bonus fun! Did you know that super coders can call the variables in their code whatever they want? If you don't like X, Y, and Z, you can also name them something really simple, such as:

name = Flex
age = 13
activity = soccer

Of course, you can also name your variables something super silly!

Like silly banana? Funky monkey? Dancing dragon? Even happy hippo?

Can you think of any more hilarious variable names to use in your code?

Coding is great fun when you get creative!

# GLOSSARY

**access:** to get at, or be able to use something

**bug:** a problem or error in coding instructions

**computer programming:** writing the coding instructions that control a computer

**debug:** find and solve a problem in coding instructions

**instruction:** information that tells us what to do

**replace:** to fill a spot with something new or different

**value:** a type of information, such as a letter, number, or word

**variable:** a special box used in computer programming to store a value

# GUIDE FOR TEACHERS, PARENTS, AND CAREGIVERS

Young children can learn the basic concepts of coding. These concepts are the foundation of computer science, as well as other important skills, such as critical thinking and problem-solving.

Variables in coding are like containers that store information. Variables help computers store a lot of information and access it quickly when running a program.

In this book, readers learn all about how variables can be used. We use the concept of writing a short book to learn the concept of assigning values to variables.

# INDEX

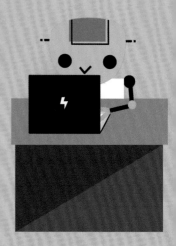